Yes!

I knew the Queen

Have fun wearing your
crown!

Jenifer Gold

Buffalo Arts Publishing

Yes! I knew the Queen. Story copyright © 2018 by Jennifer Gold.
Illustrations copyright © 2018 by Jessica Gadra.

For information, address Buffalo Arts Publishing,
179 Greenfield Drive, Tonawanda, NY 14150

Email: info@buffaloartspublishing.com

Cover design by Jessica Gadra and Melanie Schultz

ISBN 978-0-9978741-8-1
LCCN 2018945165

Acknowledgements

It's clear this book just would not be
Without the work of the following three:

Jessica Gadra for her lovely illustrations. I give her the manuscript and wait. I am always amazed and delighted.

Alex Livingston for help with layout and design.

Len Kagelmacher for his expertise and patience in answering my endless questions.

Thank you also to Melanie Schultz who chose *Yes! I Knew the Queen* as part of The Reading Project — an online reading resource utilizing an all-new, patent-pending book format. Read it now at **www.setbooksfree.org.**

To Joan,

...who first asked me this question in 1975 and delighted in encouraging many others to do the same!

Wish you were here Joan, to see what you started.

— Jennifer Gold

To Alex,

...always Alex

— Jessica Gadra

Yes!

I knew the Queen

by Jennifer Gold

Illustrated by Jessica Gadra

came here from England
Quite a long time ago.
I was asked lots of questions
People wanted to know –

Had I seen the Palace?
Did I always drink tea?
Had I met the Queen?
Was she friendly with me?

I kept saying "No!"
And shaking my head
And then an idea
Popped up instead!

Why not just tell them,
I *did* know the Queen!
And make up some tales
Of where we had been?

So here are the stories
I used to tell folks.
I think they believed me!
I thought it a joke!

"Yes, I knew the Queen,"
I would laughingly say,
"We ate cream puff pastries
The first day in May."

We liked to go shopping
In all the big stores.

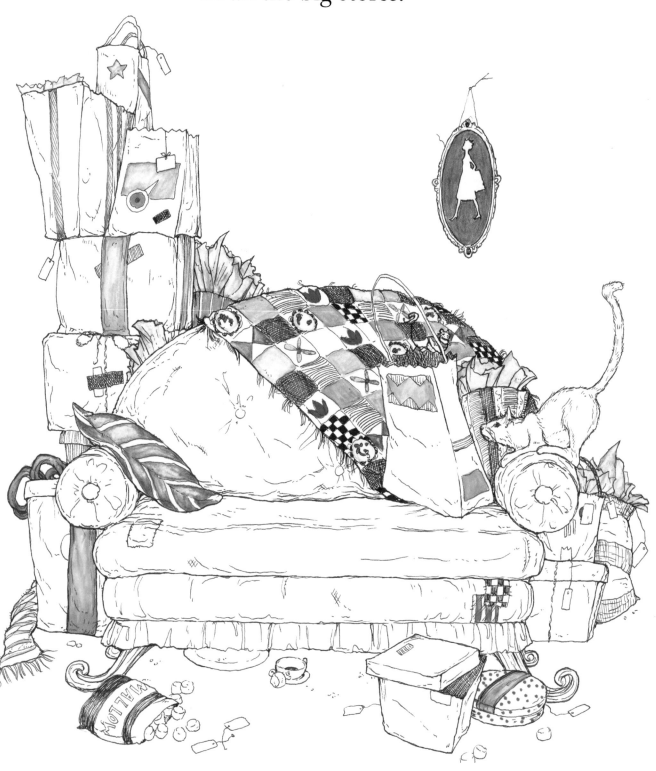

And when we were hungry

We made ourselves "s'mores!"

I rode her thin horse called
"Enchanted Fairy".

And she rode my pony
Called "Fatso Ben Hairy"!

We walked in the park

But she couldn't be seen,

So we wore big, dark glasses

And had to look mean!

We played in her attic
And tried on old crowns—
They belonged to Sir Gerald
(He's no longer around).

We looked through the trunks
Found a big bag of gems,
Then we waltzed in the dresses
But tripped on the hems!

At times we wrote postcards

And talked on the phone.

We even had email

From castle to home.

But - I haven't seen her
For quite a long time.
I grew up and traveled
And left her behind.

Often I wonder

If the Queen might be sad.

Maybe she misses

The good times we had.

So first thing tomorrow
I'll write her a note
On pink fancy paper
That's shaped like a boat.

I hope she will laugh,

Maybe she'll smile,

Recalling the fun

We had for a while.

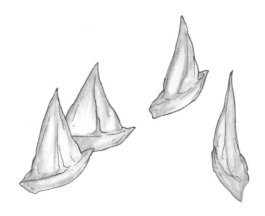

But here are two questions -
I'll leave them for you….

Do *you* think we were friends?
Is this story true?

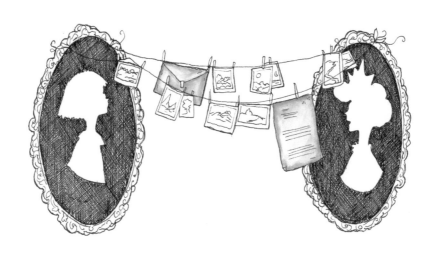

S'mores Recipe

Time to make – 10 minutes

Ingredients

- 8 sheets honey graham crackers
- One medium bar of milk chocolate broken into 8 pieces
- 8 large marshmallows

Directions

Put tinfoil (aluminum foil) on the broiler/grill pan

Halve and separate into individual squares the amount of graham crackers and put one half on the sheet of tinfoil.

Put a big piece of chocolate on each cracker

Put a marshmallow on top of each piece of chocolate

Put under the broiler/grill until the chocolate and marshmallow start to melt

Put second cracker on top of the melting marshmallow/chocolate

Squash second cracker down firmly and remove to a plate

These are delicious warm and gooey but make sure the marshmallow/chocolate mixture is not too hot before eating.

Cream Puff Pastry Recipe

Ingredients

- 1/2 cup (=1 stick or 4 ounces or 113 grams) unsalted butter, cut into pieces
- 1/2 teaspoon salt
- 1 cup all-purpose flour (= 4.5 ounces or 120 grams)
- 5 large eggs
- 1 cup water (8 fluid ounces)
- Whipped heavy cream with or without tablespoon of sugar, or can of whipped cream.

Directions

1. Preheat oven to 375 degrees. Line two baking sheets with parchment paper.

2. Put butter, salt and water in a medium pan and bring to a boil over medium heat. Quickly stir in the flour with a wooden spoon. Keep stirring until a ball of dough forms and the spoon could almost stand up in the dough ball.

3. Remove from heat and add one lightly beaten egg at a time. Stir vigorously after each egg. When dough is glossy, thick and easily molded you have enough eggs. You may not have to add all of the eggs.

4. Use a teaspoon and a dessert spoon to transfer blobs of dough to the baking tray.

5. If you need to touch the dough use a moistened finger.

6. Bake until puffs rise and are golden brown, about 30 minutes. Cool on sheets on wire racks. Can be stored at room temperature for up to 1 day.

It's probably best for an adult to help with making the puff pastry, but children can easily spoon the cream onto the two halves and then sandwich the halves together. Alternatively, they can squirt the cream into the puff balls directly from the can.

Serve immediately.

If you want to make paper boats, all you need is a packet of pink computer paper and a Web search. There are lots of sites with pictures and videos to help you.

—JG

CPSIA information can be obtained
at www.ICGtesting.com
Printed in the USA
BVHW02n0319091018
528824BV00002B/2/P